Four Feet, Two Sandals

Written by Karen Lynn Williams & Khadra Mohammed
Illustrated by Doug Chayka

Eerdmans Books for Young Readers

Grand Rapids, Michigan • Cambridge, U. K.

Text © 2007 Karen Lynn Williams and Khadra Mohammed
Illustrations © 2007 Doug Chayka

Published in 2007 by Eerdmans Books for Young Readers,
an imprint of Wm. B. Eerdmans Publishing Co.

Wm. B. Eerdmans Publishing Co.
2140 Oak Industrial Dr. NE, Grand Rapids, Michigan 49505
P.O. Box 163, Cambridge CB3 9PU U.K.

www.eerdmans.com/youngreaders

Manufactured in China

07 08 09 10 11   8 7 6 5 4 3 2 1

Library of Congress Cataloging-in-Publication Data

Williams, Karen Lynn.
Four feet, two sandals / written by Karen Lynn Williams and Khadra Mohammed;
illustrated by Doug Chayka. — 1st ed.
p. cm.
Summary: Two young Afghani girls living in a refugee camp in
Pakistan share a precious pair of sandals brought by relief workers.
ISBN 978-0-8028-5296-0 (alk. paper)
[1. Refugee camps — Fiction. 2. Refugees — Pakistan — Fiction. 3. Shoes — Fiction.
4. Sharing — Fiction.]   I. Mohammed, Khadra. II. Chayka,
Doug, ill. III. Title.
PZ7.W66655Fou 2007
[E] — dc22
2006002635

Display type set in Yolanda
Text type set in Fairfield
Illustrations created with acrylics

Gayle Brown, Art Director
Matthew Van Zomeren, Graphic Designer

For Khadra, a kindred spirit, and Zanib, who asked for a book — *K.L.W.*

For every refugee girl who has had to flee her home, leaving friends and family behind — *K.M.*

For N.B. — *D.C.*

Lina raced barefoot to the camp entrance where relief workers threw used clothing off the back of a truck. Everyone pushed and fought for the best clothes. Lina squatted and reached, grabbing what she could.

The crowd began to leave. In the dust at Lina's feet lay a brand new sandal. It was yellow with a blue flower in the middle, and when she slipped it on her foot it fit perfectly. Lina was ten, but she had not worn shoes for two years.

She looked around for the matching sandal. A girl stood nearby. She was thinner and darker than Lina, and she wore a blue and yellow sandal.

"As-salaam alaykum." Lina greeted her. "Peace be with you."

The girl only stared. She was dressed in a shalwar-kameez. Her feet were cracked and swollen, as Lina's had been when she first arrived in camp.

Suddenly the girl turned, taking the matching sandal with her.

In the morning Lina went to do the washing, wearing one beautiful sandal. She picked her way to the stream, careful to keep her sandal out of the filth. Her old shoes had been ruined on the many miles of walking from Afghanistan to Peshawar, the refugee camp in Pakistan. She had carried her brother, Najiib, no bigger than a water jug then, but just as heavy.

When she looked up from her scrubbing, the girl from yesterday was standing over her. She wore one sandal that she bent over and removed.

"Grandma says it is stupid to wear only one." She placed the sandal at Lina's feet. Then she turned and walked away.

"Wait." Lina grabbed both sandals and followed her. "I am Lina."

The girl turned slowly. "I am Feroza."

Lina held the sandals out. "We can share."

"What good is one sandal for two feet?" Feroza frowned.

"You wear them both today, and I will wear them tomorrow." Lina smiled. "Four feet, two sandals."

Feroza smiled too. She took the sandals and put them on. "Tomorrow they will be yours."

The two girls greeted each other as they carried their jugs for water the next day.
Lina put the sandals on, and they waited together in the long line.

Everyone in the camp was waiting for a new home. Mama went to meetings about being resettled. The girls stayed in Lina's tent with Ismatu and Najiib. They were careful to keep the sandals away from the two boys, for Ismatu wanted to pull at the flowers, and Najiib wanted to chew on them.

"My father and sister were killed in the war," Lina told her friend. "Mama and I had to run with Ismatu and Najiib in the night."

Feroza nodded and two tears ran down her cheek. "I have only my grandmother now."

When they did not have work to do, Lina and Feroza crept up to the windows of the school and peeked inside. The school was small with only enough room for the boys to study. The girls practiced their names in the dirt and brushed the marks away, so no one would see their mistakes.

Sometimes each girl wore one sandal. Other children pointed and giggled but Lina and Feroza did not care.

In the evenings the sky turned deep blue and the first stars began to sparkle. Lina and Feroza watched for the sliver of the crescent moon that signaled the beginning of Ramadan. They shared memories and whispered their dreams for a new home.

One morning they went to the stream and washed their sandals to keep them looking new.

"Lina, come quick," Feroza's grandmother called. "Your mother says your name is on the list."

Feroza grabbed the sandals. The two girls ran ahead to the office.

Lina stood on tiptoes and squinted at the sign.
"Mama's name! It's here! We are going to
America." She looked at her friend.

"My name is not there," Feroza said quietly.
She looked at her feet as she spoke.

Then she bent down and took the sandals off.
She handed them to Lina. "You cannot go
barefoot to America."

Feroza gave Lina a hug.

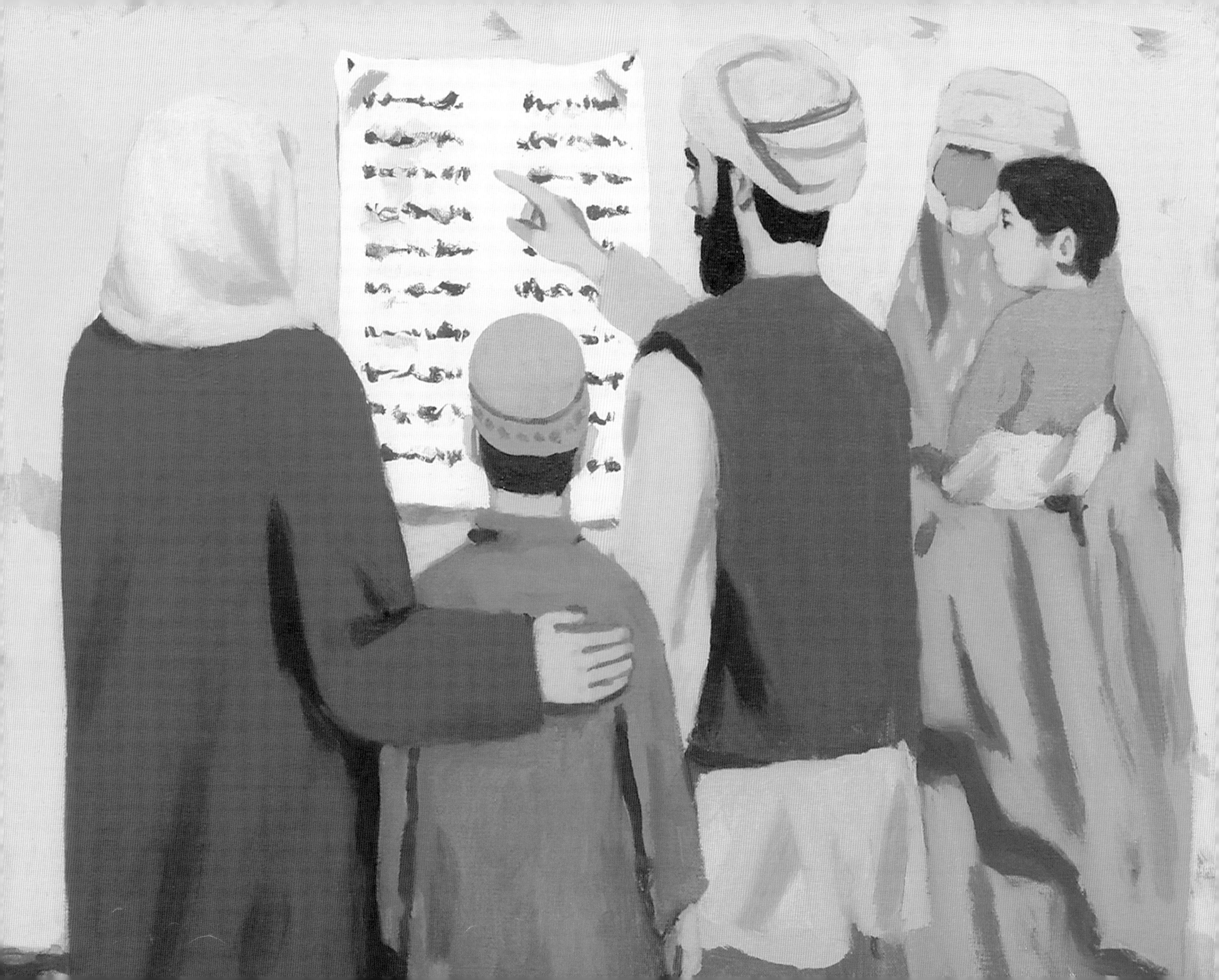

When it was time to leave, the relief worker gave Mama a large square white bag with numbers on it. "All of your important papers are in this bag," he said.

Feroza and her grandmother came to say goodbye.

Lina pointed at her feet. "Look, Mama saved her sewing money. She has bought us shoes for America."

"Real shoes." Feroza admired the new black leather.

"Here," Lina said. "It is your day to wear these." The tears in her eyes were not for the sandals.

"As-salaam alaykum," Feroza said as she took the faded yellow and blue sandals. "Peace be with you."

Lina followed the others to the bus.

"Wait!" Feroza called as she ran to her friend. "You must keep one."

She handed Lina one sandal.

"What good is one sandal?"

"It is good to remember." Feroza held up the other sandal. "Four feet, two sandals."

Lina felt the tears make a trail down her cheek. She slipped the sandal into her bag and climbed on the bus.

Feroza ran alongside as the bus began to move.

Lina leaned out the window.

"We will share again in America," she called.

Authors' Note

People who flee their country because of fear of persecution are called refugees. At the time we were writing this story, there were more than 20 million refugees worldwide. The majority of refugees are children.

This story is based on Khadra's experiences with refugees in Peshawar, a city on the Afghanistan-Pakistan border. Decades of war and instability in Afghanistan have forced millions of Afghani people to flee their homes to neighboring countries. Many of them live in makeshift camps in and around Peshawar. Some, like Lina and her family, are able to find safe haven in resettlement countries in Europe or in the United States.

Though this story is based on a camp in Peshawar, the experiences of children like Lina and Feroza are shared by refugees around the world.